# I'M JUST NO GOOD AT RHYMING

## AND OTHER NONSENSE FOR MISCHIEVOUS KIDS AND IMMATURE GROWN-UPS

WRITTEN BY Chris Harris

ILLUSTRATED BY Lane Smith

**LB**

LITTLE, BROWN AND COMPANY
NEW YORK · BOSTON

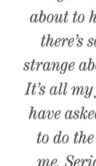

*AUTHOR'S NOTE: I am SO sorry… I realized just as I was about to hand in this book that there's something a little bit strange about the page numbers. It's all my fault—I should never have asked Leo Arden's parents to do the page numbering for me. Seriously, what is wrong with those guys?*

ABOUT THIS BOOK

The illustrations for this book were made with India ink on vellum, which was pressed onto watercolor paper to create a blotted line effect. The color, painted in oil over gesso, was scanned and added digitally on a secondary layer under the ink-line. The text was set in Century Book Condensed, and the display type is Bureau Grot Comp Bold. This book was edited by Andrea Spooner and designed by Molly Leach with art direction by Saho Fujii. The production was supervised by Ruiko Tokunaga, and the production editor was Annie McDonnell.

This book is a work of fiction. Names, characters, places, and incidents are the product of the author's imagination or are used fictitiously. Any resemblance to actual events, locales, or persons, living or dead, is coincidental.

Little, Brown and Company
Hachette Book Group
1290 Avenue of the Americas, New York, NY 10104
Visit us at lb-kids.com

Little, Brown and Company is a division of Hachette Book Group, Inc.
The Little, Brown name and logo are trademarks of Hachette Book Group, Inc.

The publisher is not responsible for websites (or their content) that are not owned by the publisher.

First Edition: September 2017

Library of Congress Cataloging-in-Publication Data
Names: Harris, Chris, 1970– author. | Smith, Lane, illustrator.
Title: I'm Just No Good at Rhyming and Other Nonsense for Mischievous Kids and Immature Grown-Ups / written by Chris Harris ; illustrated by Lane Smith.
Description: First edition. | New York : Little, Brown and Company, 2017.
Identifiers: LCCN 2016005404| ISBN 9780316266574 (hardcover) | ISBN 9780316266598 (ebook)
Classification: LCC PS3608.A78237 A6 2017 | DDC 811/.6—dc23
LC record available at https://lccn.loc.gov/2016005404

ISBNs: 978-0-316-26657-4 (hardcover), 978-0-316-26659-8 (ebook)

10 9 8 7 6 5 4 3 2 1

APS

Printed in China

*This book is dedicated to my favorite and only children, Jozy and Silas, who inspired it, and to my brilliant and beautiful wife, Hilary, who wrote this dedication for me.*
—Chris Harris

*I also dedicate this book to Chris's children, Jozy and Silas, and to his brilliant and beautiful wife, Hilary.*
—Lane Smith

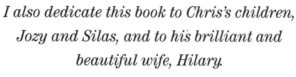

*…Um, Lane? Can't you find your own people to dedicate this book to?*
— Chris Harris

*Yeah, like maybe your own wife?*
—Molly Leach, who is Lane's own wife

*Fine. I dedicate this book to my own brilliant and beautiful wife, Molly.*
—Lane Smith

# THE DOOR

A door.

Just a door.

Nothing more than a door.

But it's there—

Where you swear

There was no door before.

And your world is this room that you're comfortable in—

But through there is everywhere you've never been.

Now the Doorman steps forward and asks, with a grin...

"Are you going out?...

...Or are you staying in?"

# I'M JUST NO GOOD AT RHYMING

I'm just no good at rhyming.

It makes me feel so bad.

I'm just no good at rhyming,

And that's why I'm so blue.


My teacher asked if I could find a word that rhymes with "hat."

"It's something that a dog might chase."

                              "Aha!" I said. "A car!"

My teacher asked if I could find a word that rhymes with "wizard."

"It's something small and with a tail."

                              "Aha!" I said. "A puppy!"

My teacher asked if I could find a word that rhymes with "wall."

"It's something you might try to catch."

                              "Aha!" I said. "A lizard!"

I'm just no good at rhyming.

I'm sorry, but it's true.

I'm just no good at rhyming,

And that's why I'm so sad.

I'm pretty good with meter,

And with spelling and with timing.

But I'll never be a poet,

'Cause I just can't rhyme words at all.

# THE ISLAND WHERE EVERYONE'S TOBY

I've been to Tahiti, I've been to Nairobi,
I've been to the Arctic, I've been to the Gobi.
The oddest place, though, that I ever did know be
The Island Where Everyone's Toby.

The first man I met there—a farmer named Toby—
Said, "Please meet my wife, who is also named Toby."
I then met their children, named Toby and Toby
And Toby and Toby and Toby.

I hadn't had dinner, so Toby sent Toby
To Toby's Food Market, where Toby sold Toby
Some prime Toby beef and some pasta al Toby
And then, for dessert, some Peach Toby.

The hour grew late, and so Toby said, "Toby!
Tell Toby that Toby can sleep next to Toby,
And Toby's bed then will be free, unless Toby
Would rather be sleeping with Toby?"

Then Toby hugged Toby and Toby hugged Toby
And Toby and Toby and Toby hugged Toby.
Then four of the Tobys hugged one other Toby
And said, "Don't forget about Toby!"

And then the next morning, I said, "Good-bye, Toby,
And farewell to Toby, and toodle-oo, Toby,
And au revoir, Toby, and adios, Toby,
And Toby and Toby and Toby…"

…And since then I've sailed all around this great globe-y,
From Roosevelt Island to Lake Okeechobee.
And yet, still, the place where my thoughts always go be
The Island Where Everyone's Toby.*

*Of course, on its sister isle, everyone's Rory…
But that is a whole other story.

# GROWN-UPS ARE BETTER (I)

Grown-ups are better than children at chess,
And cleaning and fixing and mopping a mess.
They're better at baking and frying and steaming…
But children are better at dreaming.

Grown-ups are better than children at math,
And flushing and brushing and drawing a bath.
They're better at counting and buying and paying…
But children are better at playing.

Grown-ups are better than children at sports,
And driving and working and filing reports.
They're better at pushing and pulling and lugging…
But children are better at hugging.

Grown-ups are better at most stuff, you see,
From tying a shoelace to chopping a tree.
But children are gooder and grown-ups are badder
At just about all things that matter.

# THE GOOD-CHILD TEST

I used special ink on this poem's last line

That some children see and some don't.

If you're a *good* child, then you'll read it just fine—

# ALPHABET BOOK

**A** *is for* ANTHILL

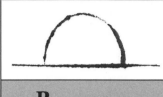

**B** *is for* BRIDGE

**C** *is for* COWBOY HAT

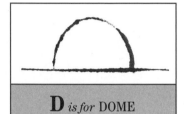

**D** *is for* DOME

**E** *is for* EGG (SLICED)

**F** *is for* FLYING SAUCER

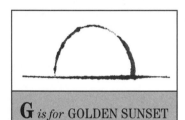

**G** *is for* GOLDEN SUNSET

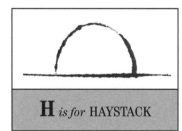

**H** *is for* HAYSTACK

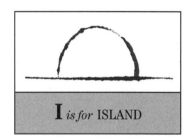

**I** *is for* ISLAND

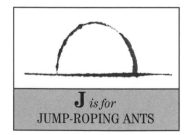

**J** *is for* JUMP-ROPING ANTS

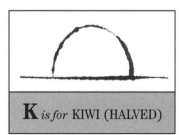

**K** *is for* KIWI (HALVED)

**L** *is for* LEX LUTHOR (HIDING)

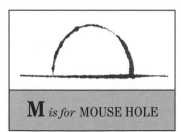

**M** *is for* MOUSE HOLE

# (BY THE LAZIEST ARTIST IN THE WORLD)

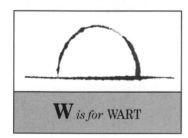

**N** *is for* NOTHING

**O** *is for* ORCHESTRA PIT

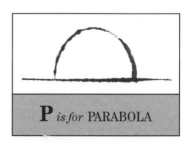

**P** *is for* PARABOLA

**Q** *is for* QUAIL
(UNDER A SERVING LID)

**R** *is for* RAINBOW

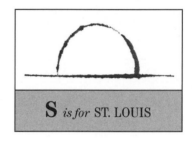

**S** *is for* ST. LOUIS

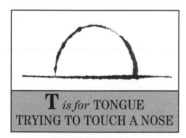

**T** *is for* TONGUE
TRYING TO TOUCH A NOSE

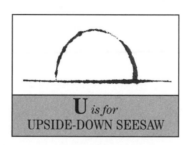

**U** *is for*
UPSIDE-DOWN SEESAW

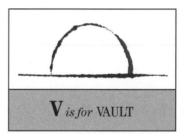

**V** *is for* VAULT

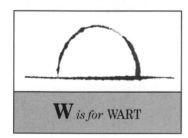

**W** *is for* WART

**X** *is for* X-ACTLY
LIKE THE LAST PAGE

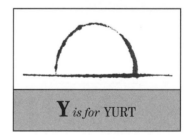

**Y** *is for* YURT

**Z** *is for* ZEBRA (DRESSED LIKE
A GHOST FOR HALLOWEEN)

# THE ONE-EYED ORR

I've never encountered a one-eyed orr.
Nor have I heard of this creature before.
But surely it's ugly and dripping with gore,
And dirty and scary and mean to its core.

I'm guessing its breath is like fish on day four,
It makes a loud noise like a wheezy whale snore,
And greenish pus oozes from every pore,
And sticky slime plops as it glops 'cross the floor.

And *that's* why I'm angry at Kylie Lepore.
She once was my friend—but no, not anymore!
So what was her insult? And why am I sore?
She kissed me and said, *"You're* the one-ey-ed orr."

# IF YOU EVER HAVE TO MEMORIZE A POEM OF TWENTY LINES OR LONGER AND DELIVER IT TO YOUR CLASS, THEN THIS IS A PRETTY GOOD CHOICE

Avocado? Avocado!

Avocado? Avocado!

Avocado? Avocado!

Avocado? Avocado!

*(tiny voice)* Avocado? *(deep voice)* **Avocado!**

*(tiny voice)* Avocado? *(deep voice)* **Avocado!**

*(tiny voice)* Avocado? *(deep voice)* **Avocado!**

*(tiny voice)* Avocado? *(deep voice)* **Avocado!**

*(fast) Avocado? Avocado!*

*(slow)* A v o c a d o ?   A v o c a d o !

*(fast) Avocado? Avocado!*

*(slow)* A v o c a d o ?   A v o c a d o !

*(whisper)* avocado? *(shout)* **AVOCADO!**

*(whisper)* avocado? *(shout)* **AVOCADO!**

*(whisper)* avocado? *(shout)* **AVOCADO!**

*(whisper)* avocado? *(shout)* **AVOCADO!**

*(face left)* Avocado? *(face right)* Avocado!

*(face left)* Avocado? *(face right)* Avocado!

*(face left)* Avocado? *(face right)* Avocado!

*(face forward)* Avocado? *(as loudly as possible)*

# TOASTED KNIGHT FOR LUNCH *AGAIN?*

Mama Dragon
Ate Sir Tom,
And gave her child
Sir Gustav.
Baby said,
"No armor, Mom—
I want him
With the crust off!"

# MY DESSERT TUMMY

I don't mean to wow.

I don't mean to flummox.

But just like a cow

I, too, have four stomachs…*

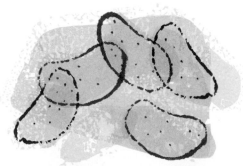

1 My veggie/fruit tummy? It isn't so big.

A twig, or a fig, or one broccoli sprig

Will make me feel full and as fat as a pig.

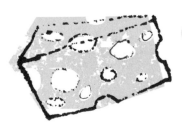

2 My meat-milk-and-bread tummy's easy to cram

With ham, or Edam, or a pb-and-jam.

Then ask if I'm full, and I'll tell you, "I am!"

3 My salty-snack tummy just hasn't felt right

Since the night that I might have had every last bite

Of a pound bag of chips. (Did it stay down? Not quite.)

4 But my dessert tummy—oh, my dessert tummy!

It's like a vast cavern for everything yummy—

A mammoth cave network for all that's non-crummy…

With alcoves for licorice, crannies for cakes,

Chambers for cherry pie, shaftways of shakes,

Tunnels for taffy and honey-nut havens,

Nooks all for cookies near rock candy cave-ins…

Fissures for fudge next to cruller crevasses,

Corridors coated with homemade molasses…

Burrows for bunnies both solid and hollowed,

Grottoes for gum (which I shouldn't have swallowed)…

Potholes of pralines, peppermint pits,

Crawlways and hallways for banana splits,

Cracker Jack cul-de-sacs, rooms of sweet rolls,

Starlight stalagmites by—yes—doughnut holes…

And plenty more niches

For all things delicious

In my dessert tummy! Oh, my dessert tummy!

It's so vast and spacious

I'm *always* voracious

In my dessert tummy! Oh, my dessert tummy!

An all-candy diet

Would not satisfy it.

Not my dessert tummy! Oh, my dessert tummy!


(And *that* is why, Mother, I'm truly not able

To take one more bite of this steamed vege-table.

But after you've thrown out what's here on my plate?

A sundae or two would be great.)


\* A scientist offered this vocal objection:
  "This 'cows have four stomachs' thing needs a correction!
  We've learned through inspections
  And many dissections,
  It's really one stomach, with four separate sections."

# THE DUEL

..............................d.b..............................

........................d..........b........................

..................d........................b................

..d........................................................b..

..b*:..............................................:*d..

..b.............:..........................:.............d..

..b..:..........................................:..d..

..p........................................................q..

# THE GECKO

If ever I find myself holding a gecko…

I'll lecko.

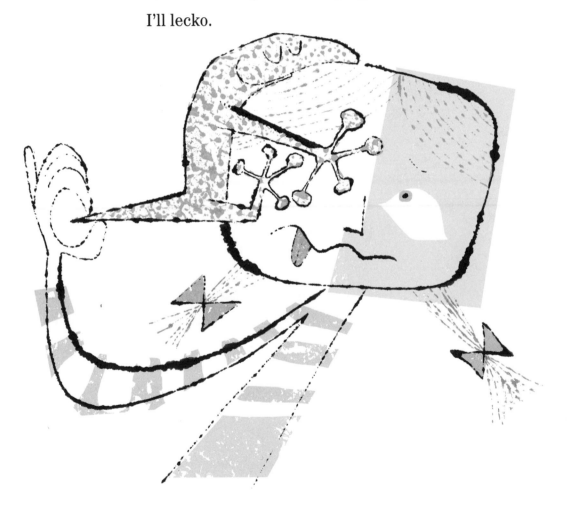

# YOU'LL NEVER FEEL AS TALL AS WHEN YOU'RE TEN

You'll never feel as tall as when you're ten.

You start out small and grow, but then

From ten you just get small again.

(Don't look at me so quizzically—

I don't mean smaller physically.

We grow into a smaller small

As women and as men.)


At ten, the world's your oyster,

It's a playland, it's a toy store,

And you're confident, and boisterous,

And nothing can't be mended.


The future looks so beautiful,

All problems seem uprootable,

And nothing's so inscrutable

Your mind can't comprehend it.

But then from ten you start to see
The limits of what you can be . . .

The *will-be*s turn to *might-be*s and the *might-be*s turn to *won't*s.
The *do-it*s turn to *try-it*s and the *try-it*s turn to *don't*s.
The *yes*es turn to *maybe*s and the *maybe*s turn to *no*s.
The *hurry*s turn to *steady*s and the *steady*s turn to *whoa*s.
The *never* turns to *hope-not* and the *hope-not* turns to *must*.
The blazes turn to embers and the embers turn to dust.
The future turns to present and the present turns to past.
The forefront turns to middle and the middle turns to last . . .

You'll never feel as tall as when you're ten.
So while you're ten, look round, and then
Remember all you see so when
You're older and your vision's poor
You'll close your eyes, and then once more
You'll see again—
What you saw then . . .
When you were tall, and ten.

# THE FROG RACE

My frog, it crossed the finish first.

You saw it with your eyes.

My frog, it crossed the finish first.

Why don't I get the prize?

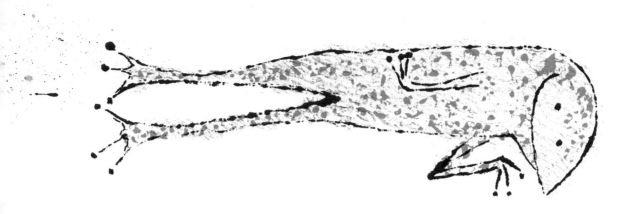

My frog, it crossed the finish first.

I didn't cheat—you know it.

Just show me where the rule book says

You're not allowed to throw it.

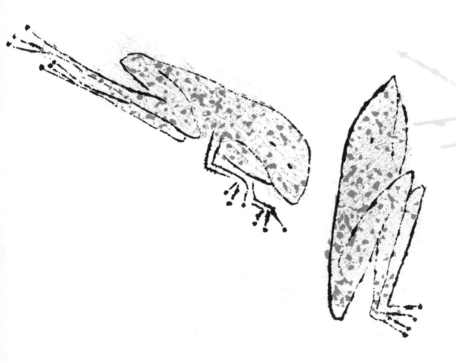

# THE LAST TIME I EVER WENT DOWN TO BREAKFAST WITHOUT MAKING MY BED

"Why should I make my bed?" I said.
"It just gets messed up again."

My mother said, "I understand,"
Picked up my eggs and raisin bran,
And tossed them in the garbage can.

"Why should I serve you food?" she said.
"You just get hungry again."

# A SHORT SAGA

The sun that night was freezing hot,
The ground was soaking dry.
I met a man where he was not
And greeted him good-bye.

With shaven beard combed in a mess
And hair as black as snow,
All bundled up in nakedness
And moving blazing slow,

He looked not more than twenty-three,
Nor less than eighty-four.
Then all at once he gradually
Let out a quiet roar.

He said, "I'll speak to you a song,
In poem without rhyme.
It's half as short as twice as long…"
"Then hurry, take your time."

And so, with breezy gravity,
And humming while he spoke,
He improvised from memory
An epic, tragic joke.

He told how many morrows past
In the unnamed land of Barrow,
The evil hero loses fast
A ring straight as an arrow.

My eyes then heard the oddest smell.
I stood up on my rear
And said, "This stranger I know well—
Begone to my arms here…

For you're my father, son of mine!"
"You're wrong, sir!" he agreed.
Repeating, then, a different line,
He spoke with plodding speed:

"I have no dad, and twice the mother.
Late at night one morn,
While in their sleep, they killed each other,
Years 'ere I was born."

I said, "Then let's have never met."
To this, he nodded "No."
"This night, I'll vividly forget.
Until back then, hello."

I dropped myself into a stand,
Did quickly dillydally,
And thus we parted, hand in hand,
And climbed up to the valley.

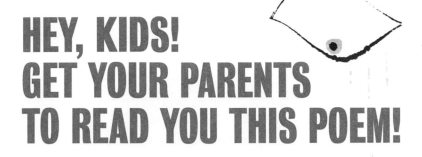

# HEY, KIDS!
# GET YOUR PARENTS
# TO READ YOU THIS POEM!

I'm your parent, and I'm so dumb,
I bite my tongue and I suck my thumb!
I try to give my fist a kiss,
But miss, and hit my nose—like this!

Go ahead, laugh at me! I don't care!
You think you're strong? Then pull my hair!
Pull my hair real hard, right now!
Do it! Do it! Do it!…Ow!

Now I'm crying, boo-hoo-hoo.
What a terrible thing to do.
I think I might boo-hoo all night.
But give me a hug…
Yes, give me a hug…
I said, GIVE ME A HUG!!!

Ah, now I'm all right.

# 'TIS BETTER...

*"'Tis better to give something*
*Than to receive it."*

If that thing's a black eye...
Then yeah, I believe it!

# THE POEM THAT'S TITLED "THE DOOR"

Read me the poem that's titled "The Door."

We'll sit on the chair by the cat on the floor,

And just like your dad and his father before,

You'll read to me some and then read to me more.

# YESTERDAY'S TOMORROW

Yesterday's tomorrow sure was better than today.

In yesterday's tomorrow, skies were blue instead of gray.

My brother never pushed me down, our beagle didn't stray,

I didn't break the faucet, and my thumb was still okay.


In yesterday's tomorrow, no one told me, "Go away."

I won our baseball game instead of caused a double play.

For dinner I had chicken tacos, not a fish fillet,

And yesterday's tomorrow ended with a mint parfait.

And now the night is falling on this downer of a day.

I had so many hopes this morning, hopes that flew away.

At least the day is almost over, leading me to say…

That I can't wait until today's tomorrow's yesterday.

# THE CYCLOPS JUST GOT GLASSES

The Cyclops just got glasses!
The Cyclops just got glasses!
(Or should I use the singular:
"The Cyclops got a *glass*"?)

He used to terrify us,
But now he skitters by us
While bullies laugh at him and shout,
"Hey, two-eyes!" as they pass.

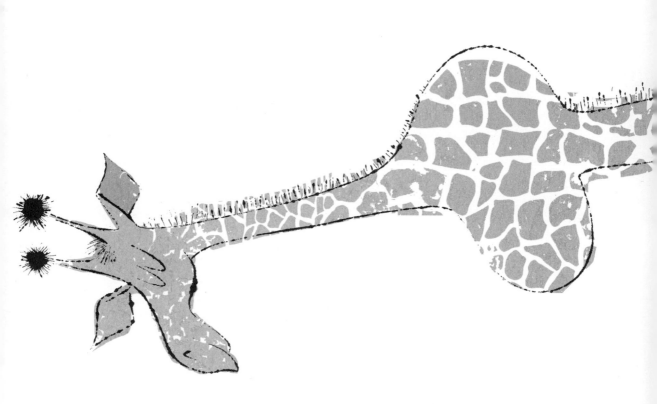

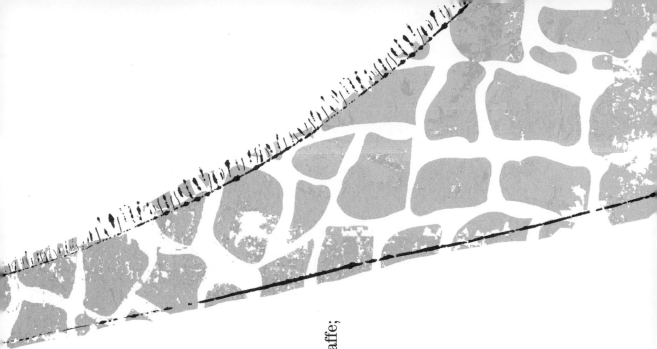

# THE HUNGRY GIRAFFE

You never should laugh at a hungry giraffe;
It takes him so long to swallow,
He may have eaten yesterday—
But he won't feel full till tomallow.

# NOTHING IS IMPOSSIBLE (THE TEACHER AND THE CHILD)

Nothing is impossible,

Child, nothing is impossible.

Every bridge is crossable.

Every tooth is flossable.

Every win is lossable.

Every worker's bossable.

Every cookie's tossable.

Every yak's a Lhasa bull.

Nothing is impossible,

Child, nothing is impossible.

*Okay, teacher, can you name something that ISN'T possible?*

No, child. Nothing is impossible.

*So, there IS something that's impossible:*
*naming something that's impossible is impossible.*

Well, um, I guess, child…

*In that case, it IS possible to name something that's impossible,*
*because naming something that's impossible is impossible.*
*But THEN, naming something that's impossible is NOT*
*impossible; it's possible, which means it IS impossible*
*to name something that's impossible, so…*

Child, I, uh…Look, I've got a lot of inspiring to do,
so get to the point. What's your question?

*Okay. If everything is possible, then is it possible*
*to name something that is not possible?*

No…Yes! No! No! Yes! Nes! Yo!
Maybe! Always! Never! AAAAAAGGHHH!!!

*(At this point the teacher's head exploded, and the child got*
*teacher brains all over her new dress. It was really, really*
*gross. And cool. The end.)*

# THE INCREDIBLE STORY OF THE DAY THE GLISTENING CITY OF SAN FRANCISCO WAS SAVED FROM CERTAIN DESTRUCTION BY A LOWLY SNAIL

Let's all gather round, and we'll hear the tale

Of the day San Francisco was saved by a snail…

…

……

………

Come on, get to it!

What? *I* can't do it—
I don't know the story. I thought *you* knew it!

Oh man. We blew it.

# THE SWEETEST LULLABY EVER (FOR PARENTS TO TELL THEIR CHILDREN)

*(say this part really softly and quietly)*

When you were a baby, so fragile and mild,

And nighttime was falling, I'd take you, my child,

Up into my arms and then gently I'd creep,

To bring you on up to the place where you sleep.

*(you're just barely whispering this part)*

I'd whisper, "I love you," with barely a sigh,

Then sing you to sleep with this soft lullaby...

*(now scream this part as loudly as you can)*

## GO TO SLEEP!!
## GO TO SLEEP!!
## GO TO, GO TO, GO TO SLEEP!!

# SLEEPY SLEEPY SLEEPY SLEEP!! NOW! NOW! NOW NOW NOW!! GOOD NIGHT!

*(now say this part super softly again)*

By then you'd be sleeping, so calm in the night.

I'd kiss you once more…and then turn out the light.

# CHOCOLATE FOR BREAKFAST

Chocolate for breakfast—tasty and sweet!

Chocolate for breakfast—oh what a treat!

But if it's for breakfast, then truly and surely,

It's not choco-*late*...It's choco-*early*!

# SOMEBODY STOLE
# MY BAGEL'S HOLE

Somebody stole my bagel's hole.

Now breakfast just isn't as fun.

It once was a treat that I wanted to eat…

…Now it's a hamburger bun.

# HOW THE
# FOURTH GRADER
# COMMUNICATES

I hate you!  You're ugly! You're dumb as a brick! You look so disgusting your face makes me sick!
I hate you! You bother me! Gross, you're the worst! If there was an ugly race, you'd come in first!
I hate you!          I hate you! I hate you the most! Disgusting!          Stupid!          Gross!
I hate you!          I hate you! I hate you the most! Disgusting!          Stupid!          Gross!
I hate you!          Stupid!          Yuck! Yuck!          Ew yuck!          Stupid!          Gross!
I hate you!          Yuck!                    Yuck!          Weirdo!          Stupid!          Gross!
I hate you!          Yuck!!                    Ew!          Gross!          Stupid!          Gross!
I hate you!          Stupid!                              Smelly!          Stupid!          Gross!
I hate you!          Stupid!!                              Ew yuck!          Stupid!          Gross!
I hate you!          Stupid! Ew!                              You're ugly!          Stupid!          Gross!
I hate you!          Stupid! Stupid!                    You smell bad!          Stupid!          Gross!
I hate you!          Stupid! Yuck! Ew!          You're disgusting!          Stupid!          Gross!
I hate you!          Stupid! Yuck!! Ew!!     Boy are you stupid!          Ew!          Gross!
I hate you!          I hate you! You disgust me! Everyone hates you.                    Trust me!
I hate you!          Don't touch me—you're covered in germs! Oh, also?          You eat worms!
I hate you! I hate you more each time you speak! You smell like a zoo! Plus, you look like a freak!
I hate you! I can't stand the dumb things you say! You're driving me crazy! Now, please go away!

# RE-VERSE

Tiresome it found I instead.
Art it find I'd that were hopes my.
Some inspire I'd that set dead
Start to end poem this wrote I.

First to last all them creatin',
Words black these typed fingers my.
Reversed lines short eight in
Backwards poem this wrote I.

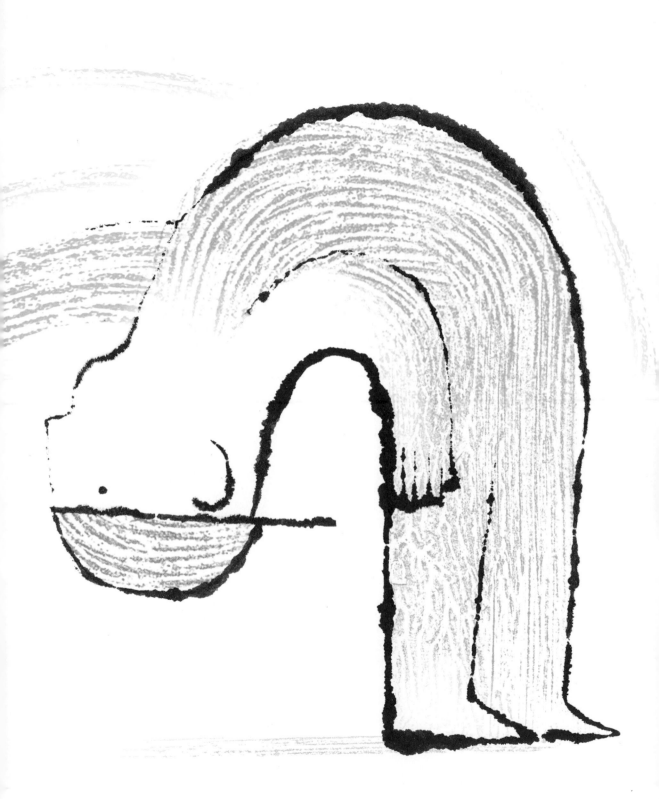

# SOMETIMES I DON'T WANT TO SHARE

Sometimes I don't want to share.

There. I said it.

Sometimes I don't want to share.

Most of the time I'm all nice and polite,

And make sure that half my dessert or delight

Goes straight to my brother without any fight.

But this time?

Just this time?

*I want every bite.*

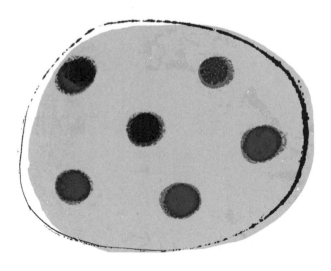

I understand sharing

Shows people we're caring.

It does. Yes it does. I would not disagree.

But why should my sibling

Get *half* what I'm nibbling

Simply because he's related to me?

Remember the tale of "The Little Red Hen"?

Or if not, "The Ant and the Grasshopper," then?

I earned this whole cookie. I got it myself.

I stepped on the counter. I climbed up the shelf.

This deep dedication should not go ignored:

I did all the work—I deserve the reward!

Yet now I'm expected to share from my plate

With this lazy and freeloading young reprobate?

You're running this house like a socialist state!

*My whole life* I've sacrificed, given, and lent.

I've suffered a tax rate of 50 percent.

I'm asking you *once* for the rules to be bent.

Just look at this cookie—please, give your consent!

Come on! I can't bear it!

Don't make me share it!

I'll share something else—here, take half my carrot!

But leave me this cookie, I'm begging you, please!

I'm pouting! I'm shouting! I'm down on my knees!

No break-y! No bite-y! No lick-y! No look-y!

I'm eating this cookie!

*I'm eating this cookie!*

You did it. You split it. The cookie's been broken,

As if all my arguments never were spoken.

And here half my cookie and I sit, defeated.

And now I don't need it.

I can't even eat it.

I'm shaking. I'm aching. What else I can do?...

I'm tired of breaking my whole life in two.

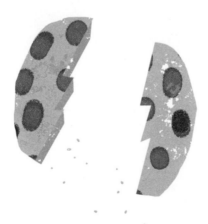

# DEEP IN THE LAND OF CA'NAROT

Deep in the land of Ca'narot,

In the shadow of Mount Garghul,

Where long ago the Elvons fought

The Orlocs for the Sword of Nool,

Freedo, Son of Toth-M'Heap,

Turned to loyal Gilterflame,

And asked outside of Proggor's Keep,

"Doesn't anyone here have a normal name?"

# INFINITY POEM

The poet who didn't know what she should write looked down at her paper—the page was all white. She thought, "I should write about something I know!" Then started her poem like so:

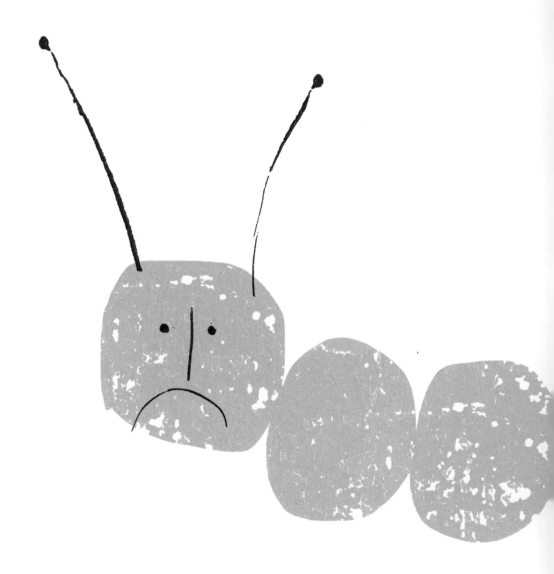

# THE UNIPEDE

The centipede's got a hundred legs
For startin' and for stoppin'.

A millipede's got a thousand legs—
A number there's no toppin'.

Me? I'm just a unipede.
A sad and lowly unipede
A lonely, only unipede
Who's sick and tired,
Yes, sick and tired,
*So* sick and tired...

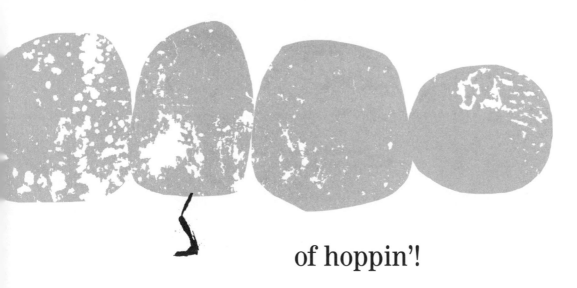

of hoppin'!

# THE RACE

Two rocks on a mountaintop, 90 BC,

Gazed far below at the scenery.

The first one said to the second, "Hey, Lee,

I'll race you on down to the edge of that sea."

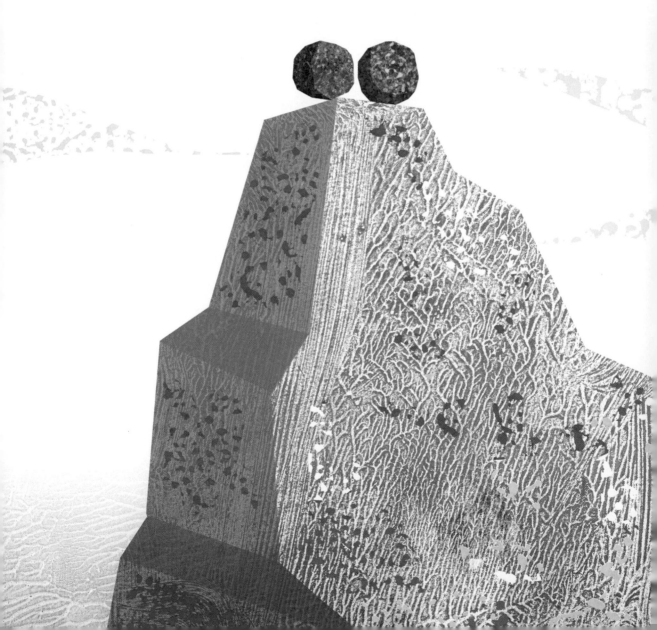

Then they sat there and sat there and sat there and sat there
And sat there and sat there and sat there.

A hundred years later a goat we'll call Phil
Knocked the first rock as he climbed up the hill.
It rolled about seventeen inches until
It came to a rest again, perfectly still.

Then they sat there and sat there and sat there and sat there
And sat there and sat there and sat there.

Three hundred years later the root of a tree
Pushed up the ground, setting some of it free.
The second rock—caught up in the debris—
Rolled down to the first. "Hello there!" said he.

Then they sat there and sat there and sat there and sat there
And sat there and sat there and sat there.

One thousand five hundred years flew by,
And neither rock shifted the width of a fly.
The second one said to the first, "Hey, Cy?
…Why don't we call it a tie?"

# FIGHT FIRE WITH FIRE?

"Fight fire with fire"?
I'm not sure you oughter.
You might have more luck
fighting fire with water.

# THE WHYDOO INSIDE YOU

You seem (or you *think* that you seem) pretty good…

But sometimes? You feel something under your hood.

A need to be naughty. A criminal craving.

A mean motivation for mass misbehaving.


If you've ever felt such a whisper inside you,

It could be you're hearing…the voice of your Whydoo!


The Whydoo inside you's a mischievous imp,

As sly as a snake and as spry as a chimp.

And just when you're trying to be extra nice,

The Whydoo will offer you rotten advice!

*(and here we pick up the pace a little…)*

Suppose you found a Magic Marker sitting in the hall…
The Whydoo whispers, "Scribble on the wall!"

Or say you have a glass of milk (your mother just refilled it)…
The Whydoo whispers, "*Psst!* What if you spilled it?"

Or say your brother's bending down to pick a four-leaf clover…
The Whydoo whispers, "Now go push him over!"

Or say you see your sleeping sister's pigtail 'neath her blanket…
The Whydoo whispers, "Hey, why don't you yank it?"

Or say your class at school was told they had to settle down…
The Whydoo whispers, "Act out like a clown!"

Or say you're eating pasta with your dear old uncle Adam…
The Whydoo whispers, "Throw a meatball at him!"

*(and now we slow it back down…)*

You say you've a Whydoo inside you, my child?
That urge to act out? That yen to run wild?
That want to act wanton? That cravin' for cursin'?
You fear that this makes you a terrible person?

Don't worry: we *all* have that down-deep desire
For pulling down pants or for playing with fire.
The Whydoo inside you does *not* mean you're awful—
In fact, you could argue, it makes you more lawful!
*For it's having bad thoughts deep down under our hood,*
*And keeping them there—why, that's what makes us good.*

# THE VALLEYS SHAPE
# THE MOUNTAINS

The valleys shape the mountains.

The shadow shapes the crescent moon.

The chill of late December

Shapes the warmth we feel in June.

So next time that you're crying,

Just remember this small rhyme;

Your sadness shapes the happiness

You'll feel again in time.

# LIVE EACH DAY LIKE IT'S YOUR LAST

"Live each day like it's your last!"

I heard my teacher cry.

And so I spent the whole day screaming,

"I'M ABOUT TO DIE!!!"

My mama wailed!

My papa railed!

My friends all wept with sorrow...

Teacher's right—that sure was fun!

I'll do it more tomorrow!

# GROWN-UPS ARE BETTER (II)

Why are grown-ups better than kids?

'Cause we got what it takes—

We never, ever, ever, ever, ever make mistaeks!

# THE SHORTEST ANACONDA

Look all through the world—from Uganda
Through Chile, Manila, Rwanda,
And on through the Tongass.
There's nothing as long as
My species: the green anaconda.

At home, I've an eight-foot-long brother,
And a seven-foot father and mother.
But me? I'm the oddest.
My length is more modest:
Five inches one end to the other.

The other snakes get up my dander,
By saying with far too much candor,
That I, when I slumber,
Look like a cucumber—
Well, that or a fat salamander.

# IN THE WORLD

My brevity's taking its toll:

When I want to go for a stroll,

For me to get hither

I can't slink or slither.

I only just flop, drop, and roll.


I can't make the shapes other snakes do—

An "O" or an "S" (though I aches to).

I can't form a torus,

Forget ouroboros,

And also caduceus (which takes two).


My life is an unending drama.

"You're still a great snake," says my mama.

But prey that I'm after

Just breaks out in laughter,

"You look like a hissing green comma!"


I might move up north, to Montana,

But never the Kenyan savannah.

It's not the warm climate—

I'm scared that some primate
Might think I'm an unripe banana!

# DISNEYLAND HAD
# NOTHING ON THIS PLACE

The greatest amusement park I've ever seen

Just went out of business 'cause business was lean.

Now forty-three rides

And eight waterslides

Are being torn down by the tear-down machine.


I know that there's nothing a person can say

To bring the park back—there just isn't a way.

Yet even I wonder

If it was a blunder

To name the park after Walt Homeworkallday.

# THE OLD WOMAN WHO LIVED IN ACHOO

There was an old woman

Who lived in a shoe—

*Bless you!*

What?

*You sneezed. Bless you!*

No I didn't. I was saying,

There was an old woman

Who lived in a shoe—

*Bless you!*

Stop it! I didn't sneeze!

*Yes you did. You said "achoo."*

No. I said "a shoe"!

*Bless you!*

A shoe! A shoe!

*Bless you! Bless you!*

I'm not saying "achoo"—

I'm saying "a shoe"!

*Wow, you're having a
really bad sneezing fit!*

Arrrrgh! Okay, fine:

There was an old woman

Who lived in a certain object

One wears on one's foot when—

*BOO!!!*

AAAHH! Why did you scare me?

*That's how you get rid of the sneezes.*

No, that's if you hiccup.

*If you what?*

Hiccup! Hiccup!

*BOO!!! BOO!!! Are your hiccups gone now?*

No! I mean, yes! I mean, I never had

them. AHH! I am so mad right now!

*At who?*

At you!

*Bless you!*

AAAARRRRRGHH!

# THE LITTLE HURTS

Learn to love the little hurts

That lesser folks have dreaded.

For every wrong

Will make you strong

If you will only let it.

The slips, the trips

The busted lips

The tendon rips

The painful grips

The scares, the yips

The towels as whips

The broken hips

The needle tips

The shower drips

The failed friendships

The claws, the clips

The jealous snips

The hurtful quips

The backward flips

The music skips

The bandage strips

The canine nips

The pinching zips

The drops, the dips

The cracks, the chips…

Learn to love each little hurt—
Find joy in getting through it.
(And when you learn?
Then please return,
And tell me how you do it!)

# WHAT HAPPENED TO US MONSTERS?

What happened to us monsters? Man, we used to be so fierce!
But everything's been different since we've gotten up in years.

Count Dracula—remember him? Nocturnal, pale, and tall?
He swore off blood—he says he's watching his cholesterol.

The Wolf Man bought a hat to cover his receding hair,
And slept right through the last full moon in his reclining chair.

The Wicked Witch gave up her broom—"It's too unsafe," she said.
She still goes out (to bingo games!), but takes the bus instead.

The Cyclops got a bifocal. Medusa's snakes went gray.
The zombies only moan that they want "brans" to eat all day.

The Blob was told to watch his weight, while Bigfoot has the gout.
The Human Fly has maggots now. The dragon's fire went out.

# (THE MUMMY'S LAMENT)

Ol' Dr. Jekyll just plays chess each night with Mr. Hyde,
While Frankenstein's a no-show since he went and got a bride.

What happened to us monsters? Man, we used to terrorize!
But now we're more concerned with rest and proper exercise.

I used to think that nothing was as scary as my curse.
But now I see that growing old is much, much, much, *much* worse.

I guess I'll go on home—I can't believe how you've all slipped!
If any monsters change your minds? Come get me in my crypt.

# THE REMARKABLE AGE

Ah, what a remarkable age that you're in:

Right now you're the oldest that you've ever been—

And yet, you will never be this young again.

So dance, and be happy! Greet life with a grin!

You've the best of both worlds, youth and wisdom, within.

# JUST BECAUSE I'M A TURKEY SANDWICH AND SOME CHIPS DOESN'T MEAN I DON'T HAVE FEELINGS TOO, YOU KNOW!

I know you love breakfast;

I hear what you say:

"It's the most important meal of the day!"

But I'm your *lunch*—

your midday meal…

How do you think that makes *me* feel?

# HEY, WE FINALLY FOUND SOMEONE WHO KNOWS THAT STORY ABOUT THE SNAIL WHO SAVED SAN FRANCISCO!

'Twas late one December…
Or was it July?
There once was a woman,
Or maybe a guy—

(Well, this much I know:
It was one or the other.
(Or was it a kid? (Or a dog?
(Or my mother?))))

And then…*something happened*!
And then…*something more*!
Then just after that…
*Something happened before!*

Then the crab from Miami—
No, lobster from Boston—
No, scallop from Reno—
No, oyster from Austin—

My point is, that April—
Or was it September…?
You know what? Forget it.
I just can't remember.

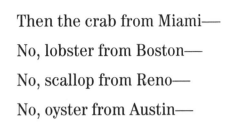

## EIGHT

Leo's mom and dad were great.

They never made him clean his plate.

At night, they let him stay up late.

In no way were they second rate.

Except in one, which I'll relate:

They both forgot to teach him…

**8**

"Eight?" you ask. "What do you mean?"

I mean that he knew seventeen

And all the other numbers too—

Like four and six and nine he knew.

But somehow, by some twist of fate,

He'd never even *heard* of eight.


And things were bound to stay that way

Until the dreaded fateful day

That little Leonardo Arden…

Found himself in kindergarten.


Said the teacher, "Is there any

Student who can say how many

Fingers I have? What amount?"

Leo then stood up to count:

"One, two, three, four, five, six, seven,
Nine, and ten—you have eleven!"

Students laughed. The teacher frowned.
Who *was* this wee obnoxious clown?
Eleven fingers? What a fool!
She said, "See me after school!"

The teacher told him, "Leo Arden,
Now that you're in kindergarten,
You must be a better student—
Not so impish, or impudent.
Trust me, you can't act this way
All twenty-four hours of the day."

Leo said, "I *do* respect you.
Still, I feel I must correct you:
'Twenty-four' you just did scold me...
That's not what you *should* have told me.
For I'm certain, dear Miss Flowers,
Each day's twenty-*six* full hours."

(Here you might say, "Hey, that's new!
Why was Leo off by *two*?
Why would that boy ever say,
Twenty-*six* hours make a day?"
The explanation's clear and clean:
If there's no eight, there's no eighteen!
(And twenty-eight is also gone,
And thirty-eight, and on, and on…
In fact, the higher Leo counted,
All the more his problems mounted.))

Leo's teacher thought, "This terror
Made a *second* counting error…
Such bizarre enumeration
Calls for an investigation!"

So she asked him, "Leo, dear,
Don't you think this quarter here
Is worth, in pennies, twenty-five?"
Leo laughed, "Oh, man alive!
I'm sorry, teacher, no offense:
A quarter's twenty-*seven* cents."

Taking note of Leo's answer,

Teacher then said, "Dasher, Dancer…

Reindeer pulling Santa's sleigh—

What's their number? Can you say?"

Leo proudly answered, "Nine!

…Or ten when Rudolph's in the line."


And so his answers *all* seemed queer:

"Thirteen months are in a year."

"I count *nine* sides on this stop sign."

"A 'Z' is letter twenty-nine."

"We've fifty-five United States."

All these he said, not knowing eights!

But now Miss Flowers had an inkling,

Why this boy had such odd thinkling…

On the board she drew an

**8**

"What is this shape that skaters skate?"

Poor Leo said, "A lovely bow?

A two-leaf clover? Man of snow?

A pair of eyes? Or could it be,

You drew sideways infinity?"

His teacher, then, at last could tell

That little Leo, he *meant* well.

This fact just wasn't in his brain.

And so she said, "May I explain

That there's a number I'll define

As more than seven, less than nine…?"


And Leo, for his mind was nimble,

Soon did grasp this missing symbol.

"Eight!" he said. "Well, that means then

Our toes and fingers number ten!

And Santa has just *eight* reindeer!

And only *twelve* months make a year!"

The teacher smiled and said, "You're right!

You've got it! Now go home, good night."

And thus concludes the thrilling fate

Of Leo…who knew naught of eight.

# EPILOGUE

Now you may find your hands are wringing
At the thought of such upbringing—
"How could parents ever be
So awful as to teach him three
And six and two but never eight?
Such parenting's inadequate!
How'd his mom and dad forget?
Had they not learned their numbers yet?
Or were they too into their pet?
Too worried about household debt?
Too focused on the alphabet?
Distracted by the Internet?"

Well, blame the 'rents if you insist,
But countless numbers *do* exist.
One thousand, fifty, seventeen,
And all the numbers in between.
So many we're told, "Don't forget!"
That who can blame them if they let
One slip their minds? (Oh no, not me.
For I did something worse, you see.
Or if not worse, at least no better:
*My* kids didn't learn one *letter*!
When they were little, long ago,
I forgot to teach them "O."
An orange they just called a *range*.
From there, it got more and more strange.
They'd *pen* their eyes after a nap.
And then they'd wash their hands with *sap*…
They tried to sail out on a *bat*.
When it got cold, they wore a *cat*.
And lots of other awful stuff.
I'd tell you more, but that's enough.)

# THE SECRET OF MY ART

"It's a beautiful whale," my teacher declared.
"This drawing will get a gold star!"

"It's a beautiful whale," my father declared.
"Your talents will carry you far!"

"It's a beautiful whale," my mother declared.
"What a wonderful artist you are!"

Well, maybe it *is* a beautiful whale…
But I was trying to draw a guitar.

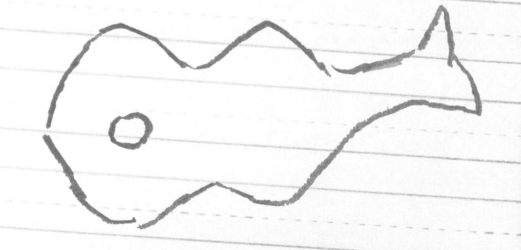

# THE POEM THAT'S TITLED "THE POEM THAT'S TITLED 'THE DOOR'"

Read me the poem that's titled "The Poem That's Titled 'The Door.'"

We'll sit on the chair by the cat on the chair by the cat on the floor,

And just like your dad and his father before and his father before,

You'll read to me some

    and then read to me,

      read to me,

        read to me more.

The night that Michael's house burned down,

He wasn't around—he was out of town.

"Boy, am I lucky, so lucky, so lucky.

Boy, am I lucky!" he said.

**LUCK**

Janey caught a violent flu,

Just after her trip to the zoo was through.

"Boy, am I lucky, so lucky, so lucky.

Boy, am I lucky!" she said.

The car that broke Sue's legs by chance

Happened to be an ambulance.

"Boy, am I lucky, so lucky, so lucky.

Boy, am I lucky!" she said.

They all say they're lucky—Mike, Janey, and Sue—

But I have my house, and I don't have the flu,

And I have two legs that are still good as new,

So if that's really luck, then NO THANK YOU!

I'll stay unlucky, unlucky, unlucky.

I'll stay unlucky, I say!

# I'M SHY ON THE OUTSIDE

I'm shy on the outside, but inside my head?
I'm not at all shy—I'm outgoing instead.

I'm chatty, I'm witty, I'm often hilarious,
Funny and friendly and downright gregarious.

Ask me about me—I'll say, "I'm a cutup!
Sometimes? I can't even get me to shut up."

Even though out here I'm minimal-worded,
Deep down inside? I am *so* extroverted!

I'm the life of the party here under my skin.
So keep knocking—
Someday I might let you in.

# THE LEMONADE STAND STAND

*Lemonade stand! Lemonade stand!*
*Step right up! Get your fresh lemonade stand!*

Hi there! You're thirsty? Oh sorry, no dice.

I've no lemonade. I don't even have ice.

Nope, NO lemonade—I sell lemonade STANDS.

So sorry this stand stand can't meet your demands…

Lemonade stand! Lemonade stand!

Look at these stands—they're all crafted by hand!

I'm telling you all, it's a great opportunity,

Serving refreshments to your own community.


Hi there! You say you're exhausted and hot,

And looking for something that might hit the spot?

You think I can help? I cannot! I CANNOT!

I'VE NO LEMONADE! It's the stands that I've got.


But *if* you've got talent, if you've got the gumption,

Then come buy a stand and make coin off consumption!

Oh, hi! Can I help you? Would *you* like a stand?

You say that you'd love a cold drink in your hand?

Well, WHAT ARE YOU, BLIND?! See the sign I displayed?
I'M SELLING STANDS HERE! I DON'T SELL LEMONADE!!

Lemonade stand! Lemonade stand!
Somebody, please! Buy a lemonade stand!

Oh, hi! Can I help you? What? You and your daughter
Were lost in the desert twelve days without water?
You'll die without drink? Aw…SCRAM! GET OUT! BEAT IT!!
If you want a stand, though, your search is completed.

You won't find a better stand stand in the land—
Whatever your stand need, I've got it on hand!
(And this lemonade stand stand, you ask, came from where?
From the lemonade stand stand stand—right over there!)

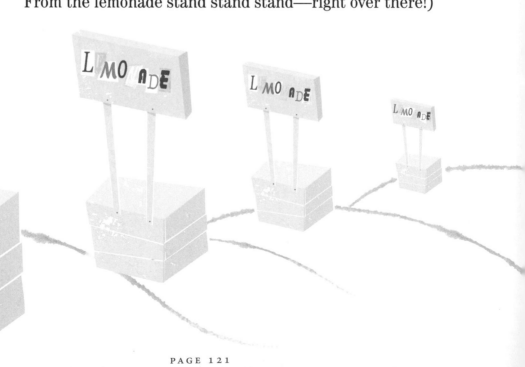

# I LOVE QUIET

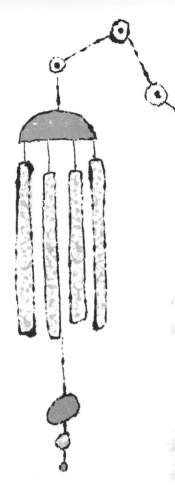

I love quiet: gentle rains,
Leaves that brush on windowpanes,
Distant birds in morning light,
Children sleeping through the night.

I love calm. Do you agree?
You do? Then will you join with me?
Softly say this, even sigh it—
Whisper with me, "We love quiet."

*"We love quiet…"* Oh, what fun—
Now I'm not the only one!
See, so many girls and boys
Would rather fill the world with noise.
Quiet-lovers should be prouder…
Let's stand up, and say it louder:

*"We love quiet…!" That's* the spirit!
We exist—the world should hear it!

Quiet-lovers, let's be strong!
We've been silent far too long!
Now's the time to take our stands—
If you love quiet, clap your hands!
Clap your hands and stomp your feet!
Stomp and cheer and then repeat.
Clap and stomp and cheer and say,
**"We love quiet! Yay! Hooray!"**

*"We love quiet! Yay! Hooray!"*
Now they hear us! More, I say!
Quiet-lovers, give a roar!
Bang a drum! Now slam a door!
In a car? Here's something! Try it:
*HONK IF YOU LOVE BEING QUIET!*
Shout until we get our way,

*"WE LOVE QUIET!*
*YAY! HOORAY!*
*WE LOVE QUIET!*
*YAY! HOORAY!*
*WE LOVE QUIET!*
*YAY! HOORAY!*
*WE LOVE QUIET!*
*YAY! HOORAY!*
*WE LOVE QUIET!*
*YAY! HOORAY!*
*WE LOVE QUIET! YAY!*

*HOORAY…!"*

(And on we'll go, just shy of violence,
Shouting in the name of silence.)

# TWO ROADS

Two roads diverged in a wood, and I—
I took the one less traveled by…
Since then I've been completely lost.
Thanks for nothing, Robert Frost!

# JACK SPRAT (UPDATED)

Jack Sprat could eat no fat.

His wife could eat no lean.

He lived to be one hundred three;

She died at seventeen.

# ROLLER COASTER + EARTHQUAKE

I hopped into the coaster ride,

Just as the ground began to shake.

"This will be insane!" I cried.

A roller coaster AND earthquake…?


The ground lurched LEFT as the coaster went *RIGHT*,

The ground rose UP as the coaster went DOWN,

The ground DROPPED DOWN as the coaster GAINED HEIGHT,

And LEFT went the coaster as *RIGHT* went the ground.

Everyone seems to agree

That earthquake was a crazy thrill.

Everyone, that is, but me—

I felt like I was sitting still.

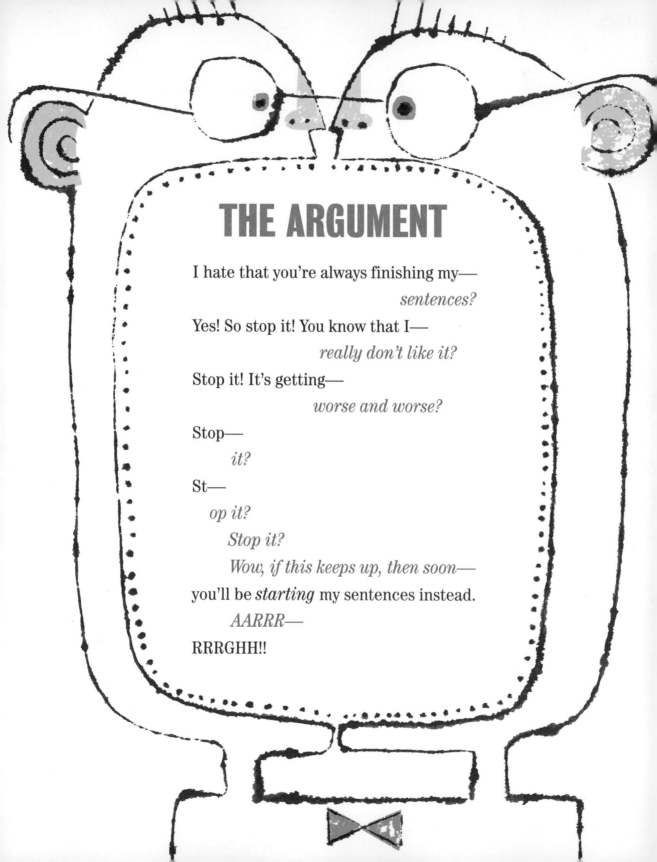

# THE ARGUMENT

I hate that you're always finishing my—
*sentences?*
Yes! So stop it! You know that I—
*really don't like it?*
Stop it! It's getting—
*worse and worse?*
Stop—
*it?*
St—
*op it?*
*Stop it?*
*Wow, if this keeps up, then soon—*
you'll be *starting* my sentences instead.
*AARRR—*
RRRGHH!!

# TRAPPED!

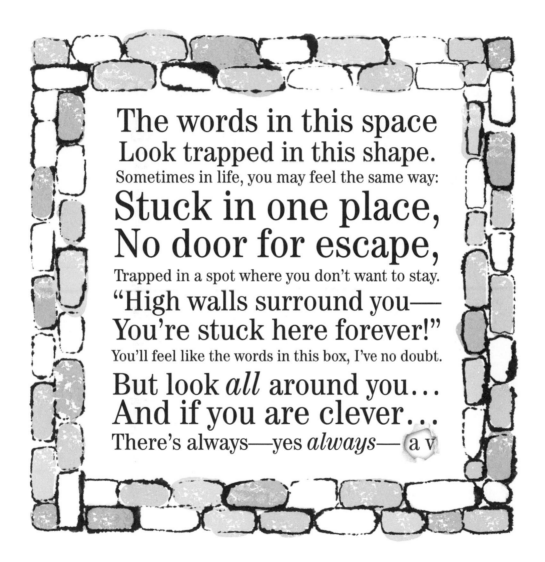

The words in this space
Look trapped in this shape.
Sometimes in life, you may feel the same way:
Stuck in one place,
No door for escape,
Trapped in a spot where you don't want to stay.
"High walls surround you—
You're stuck here forever!"
You'll feel like the words in this box, I've no doubt.
But look *all* around you…
And if you are clever…
There's always—yes *always*—a v

# UNFAIR RIDDLE #1

I'm not an egg, but I have a shell.

And yellow and white within me dwell.

No, I'm not an egg, although I'm round.

And on a farm I'm often found.

What am I?

(Oh, ignore that part. It's definitely an egg.)

(What? I said it *wasn't* an egg?

Answer: An egg.

# UNFAIR RIDDLE #2

I have ten legs, but I usually fly.

I'm harder than rock, but sweeter than pie.

I'm something you listen to every day.

The bigger I get, the less I weigh.

What am I?

Answer: A porcupine who likes to make up lies about himself.

a way to get out!

# UNFAIR RIDDLE #3

What am I?

Answer: A riddle, you dummy. It says so right there in the title.

# THE INVISIBLE HORSE

Will anyone buy
This invisible horse?
You ask, "Is he real?"
Of course! Of course!
He's standing right here,
So what you can do
Is reach out your hand
Like this, and—

*MOO!*

Oh my.
I think
I messed up
Somehow…
Will anyone buy
This invisible *cow*?

# GOOD THINGS

Good things come

To those who wait…

’Cause those who don’t

Get all that’s *great*.

**JACK**
You're stupid.

> **JANE**
> You're stupid!

**JACK**
You're stupider!

> **JANE**
> You're stupidest!

**JACK**
You're stupid times ten!

> **JANE**
> You're stupid times a hundred!

**JACK**
You're stupid times a thousand!

> **JANE**
> You're stupid times a million!

**JACK**
You're stupid times a billion!

> **JANE**
> You're stupid times a trillion!

**JACK**
You're stupid times infinity-minus-one!*

> **JANE**
> You're stupid times infinity!

# STRATEGIC BLUNDER

JACK

…Darn it.

\* That scientist just had another reaction:
"You can't make infinity *less* through subtraction."
I'd explain how we know it,
But I'm just a poet—
With numbers? I understand only a fraction.

# THE WORLD'S BEST OFFER

I'm in Dad's arms. The night is clear.
His collar rubs against my ear.
I hear the wind sift through a tree.
I hear the World—it calls to me...

*"Why are you waiting, kid? How can you rest?*
*You're wasting your time sitting there on his chest!*
*You've too much to do and you've too much to see;*
*My secrets are yours—if you'll just run to me!*
*I've deserts to dance on! Oceans to dive in!*
*Mountains to prance on and pastures to thrive in!*
*Strangers for meeting! Caves for exploring!*
*Freeways for speeding and airways for soaring!*
*High-rise construction! Shipwreck recovery!*
*Harvest production! Diamond discovery!*
*Turbines and combines with power untold!*
*Castles of silver and cities of gold!*
*My treasures are waiting for you to come see!*
*So hurry up, kid, hurry up—run to me!"*

The wind dies down. I know it's true.
I've much to see. And be. And do...

Dad's breath is warm. I feel his sighs.
The night is still. I close my eyes.

There's plenty of time for all that stuff.
Tonight, right here is world enough.

# THE NURSERY RHYME "LITTLE BOY BLUE," WITH SOME WORDS REPLACED BY DELICIOUS GREEK FOOD

Little Boy Blue, come blow your hummus.

The pita bread's in the meadow,

the cow's in the yogurt—*Sorry, Chris, I have to stop you right there. This poem is too ridiculous. I don't think I can illustrate it. Can you try writing a different poem instead? Thank you! —Lane*

Um, okay…

# NEVER SWITCH YOUR LAUNDRY DETERGENT WITH YOUR DISHWASHER DETERGENT

My forks are all fluffy, both handles and tines,

While all of my underwear sparkles and shines—*Nope! Sorry, still too ridiculous! Write something else, please! —Lane*

# THE ABDOMINAL SNOWMAN

A creature, made of ice and snow!

It trundles 'cross the frozen lake,

And bellows, in a fearsome show,

"Mommy! I've a tummy ache!"—*NO! NO! NO!*
*I'm not going to illustrate that! Please try*
*again and remember: LESS RIDICULOUS!*


# NOTHING RHYMES WITH DUTHING

Nothing rhymes with—*NO! NO! NO!*
*TOO RIDICULOUS!! I WILL*
*NOT ILLUSTRATE IT.*

*Maybe something about a*
*monster under the bed instead?*

# THE MONSTER UNDER MY BED ~~INSTEAD~~ IS DEAD

The monster under my bed is dead.

I should be shouting, "Oh boy!"

And out celebrating

And stand-up ovating

And leaping (and weeping!) with joy.


The monster under my bed is dead.

So why am I not more elated?

There's a brand-new monster in my closet—

He's the one who ate it.

# PICTURE PUZZLE!

Can you find and circle *6* differences between these two pictures?

*Answer: No, you cannot. They are the exact same picture.*

# TEN GINORMOUS HIPPOS JUMPED ON A BED

Ten ginor—

OH NO WE JUST
BROKE THE BED
LET'S GET OUT
OF HERE!!!!

# I DON'T LIKE MY ILLUSTRATOR

I must confess that I don't like my poems' illustrator.

They told me, "Lane is great!" but man, I really think I hate her!

I swear that I drew better when I was a second-grader!

You won't believe my endless list of reasons to berate her:

I told her, "Draw a staircase!" But she drew an escalator!

I told her, "Draw a circle!" But she drew me the equator!

I told her, "Draw a crocodile!" She drew an alligator!

I'm sorry if this criticism starts to irritate her.

But if she doesn't step it up, I'll get somebody greater.

But I've been smart—for as of now, I haven't even paid her.

(I wonder what she'll draw right here? I guess I'll find out later.)

THIS IS WHAT CHRIS HARRIS LOOKS LIKE

ALSO, FOR THE RECORD I'M A HE NOT A SHE!

# YES MEANS NO AND NO MEANS YES...

Suppose one day, while you're at play,

A bully comes up and starts to say,

"Yes means no and no means yes...

Do you want me to hit you?" Well, what's your guess?


Oh, what a question! Oh, what a lout!

At first, it seems, there's no way out.

If you say, "No," he'll say, "You twit,

*No* means *yes*"—then you'll get hit!


But then if you say, "Yes," he'll go,

"Sure, it's true that *yes* means *no*...

But then that *no* means *yes*," he'll say.

And so he'll hit you anyway!

That boy's got you in quite a pickle.

And if you're hit? It sure won't tickle.

So what to do? What's best? What's worst?

The answer is simple: *Hit him first!!*

## AN APOLOGY

This last poem ended with talk about something
That shouldn't be done. No, in fact, it's a dumb thing.
Others have said this, but let me repeat it:
Treat folks the way that *you'd* like to be treated.*

* Unless the way that you like being treated is to
be tickled. Please do not ever tickle me.
Especially my feet.

# I'M ALWAYS HAPPY IN MY ROOM

I'm always happy in my room—
My room is like a bigger me.
I'm calm and warm and free of gloom,
Surrounded by my property.

My chair is where I dare to dream.
My bed, right there, is…

Hey, what happened to my bed?

It looks totally broken.

It's like somebody—or maybe even a *bunch* of
somebodies—were jumping on it, or…

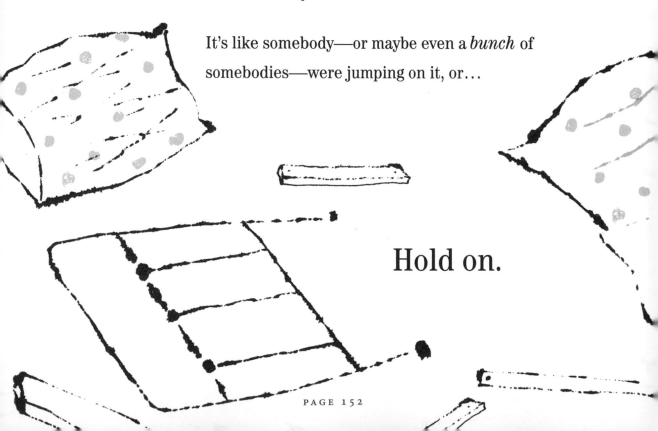

Hold on.

WERE THOSE HIPPOS JUMPING ON MY BED?! THIS IS MY ROOM! WHO LET THE HIPPOS IN HERE?! I AM SO *NOT* HAPPY RIGHT NOW! LET'S GO GET THEM!

# THE RULES OF "TIC"

"Tic" is just like "tic-tac-toe,"

But you only have to get *one* in a row.

Let's play, and see who's best and worst!

Just one condition: I go first.

# THE POEM THAT'S TITLED "THE POEM THAT'S TITLED 'THE POEM THAT'S TITLED 'THE DOOR'""

Read me the poem that's titled "The Poem That's Titled
'The Poem That's Titled 'The Door.'"
We'll sit on the chair by the cat on the chair by the cat on
the chair by the cat on the floor,
And just like your dad and his father before and his father
before and his father before,
You'll read to me some and then
read to me,
  read to me,
   read to me,
    read to me,
     read to me more.

# JUST BE YOURSELF

"Just be yourself," they always say.

But I, your dad, forgot today.

This morning, getting out of bed,

I wound up being YOU instead.

Since I'm already you…Let's see…

Just today…Can YOU be ME?

Don't worry, now—I'll eat your lunch,

And play your games, and drink your punch,

And mostly (for you do it well),

I'll run around and scream and yell—

In every way I'll dutifully

Be you—and be you beautifully!

And meanwhile you've got such a treat

In store for you today, my sweet,

For all the things that *I'd* have done,

*You* get to do today (what fun!)…

Just mow the lawn, take out the trash,

Fold my laundry, make some cash,

Run my errands, clip my toes,

Fix that door that doesn't close,

Call the doctor, sort the mail,

Throw out all the bread that's stale,

Take my car in for repairs,

Get in shape by running stairs,

Wish for time to take a snooze,

Worry 'bout what's on the news,

Make the bed, replant the tree,

Finish this poem, _____,

_____,

_____,

_____,

_____!

# THE INCREDIBLE BARGAIN

Last night, I was walking down the street when a guy came up to me and said, "Hey, *psst*, you wanna buy an invisible diamond?"

Naturally I was a little skeptical, so I said, "Do you actually *have* an invisible diamond?"

"Sure," he said, and held it up between his fingers. Now of course I couldn't see it, but I *could* see how far apart his fingers were, and let me tell you—that invisible diamond was *big*!

"How much?" I asked.

"Fourteen bucks," he said. Fourteen bucks? For a diamond? That big? With incredible powers of invisibility? Well, I know a bargain when I see one. I paid him the money, he put the diamond in my bag, and I hurried off.

I'd gotten about ten steps away when I realized: "I've been scammed! Ripped off! Bamboozled!" Yes, that guy had tricked me! But I was not about to let him get away with it.

I hurried back, grabbed the man by his jacket, and told him, "I gave you a twenty-dollar bill, and you only gave me *four* dollars back. The correct change for fourteen dollars should be *six* dollars!"

Boy, you should have seen the look on that guy's face! Needless to say, he quickly gave me the two dollars he owed me, and I walked off, proud that I hadn't fallen for his little trick.

I mean, what did he think I am, some kind of fool?

# I'M OLD FOR MY AGE

I'm old for my age, but I'm tall for my height.

I'm big for my size; for my weight, though, I'm light.

My voice must have left, since my words are not right.

Just bid me "Hello," and I'll greet you "Good night!"

# HOW TO DESIGNATE AN UNGULATE

A one-humped camel's a dromedary;

A two-humped camel's a Bactrian.

A three-humped camel's imaginary,

And four humps? Completely non-factrian.

# THE WAY WE'RE ALL THE SAME

Some folks are doers and some folks are thinkers.

Some folks are eaters and some folks are drinkers.

Some folks are givers and some folks are takers.

Some are destroyers while others are makers.

Some folks like veggies and some folks like meat.
Some love the forest and some love the street.
Some don't like others, while others love some.
Some like the quiet, and some like to drum.

But we're *all* in trouble—'cause we all might die—
If great white sharks ever learn to fly.

# OUT ON THE FARM ON A SATURDAY NIGHT

Out on the farm on a Saturday night,

Young Danny McNair started up with a fright,

Ran straight to his father, old Farmer McNair,

And cried, "There's a terrible noise out there!"


The two of them listened, and soon heard the moaning:

**OOW OOW**

Some nightmarish creature was groaning.
The farmer then said with a deep, furrowed brow:
"It sounds like we've got an upside-down cow."

So down to the pasture went farmers McNair
And there was the cow with her hooves in the air,
And her head and her back and her tail on the ground,
Just making that terrible "OOW OOW" sound.
The father said, "Danny, we have to upright her."
And Danny agreed. "I just wish she was lighter."

So Pa took the chuck side and Dan took the round.
They spit in their hands, dug their heels in the ground,
They heaved and they ho'ed and they tried and they tried,
And soon they had gotten the cow on her side…

Said the poor troubled cow as she lay there.
Danny McNair said, "We can't let her stay there!"

So Pa took the brisket and Dan took the flank.
They gave her a push and a shove and a yank,
And Dan put his shoulder right into her brand,
And all of a sudden, they got her to stand…

But then (in a case of misovercorrection),
The cow toppled down in the other direction!

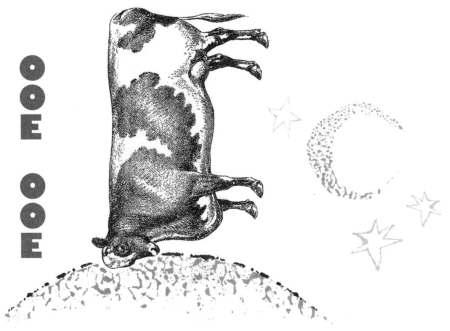

The poor cow, from the meadow, she cried,
Depressingly stuck on her opposite side.
Old Farmer McNair said, "We have to reset her…
Let's do it again—but this time? Do it better!"

So Pa took the rib eye and Dan took the skirt.

They pushed till it stung and they shoved till it hurt.

Then finally, FINALLY all were delighted

To find that the cow was correctly uprighted!

## MOO MOO

Lowed the cow. "That's more like it!" they said,

Returned to the farmhouse, and went back to bed.

And Dan, in his bed, was so glad that he heard

Almost no sound at all—just the call of a bird,

Hanging out in the barn, going,

## OHM OHM OHM

And he went back to sleep in his farmhouse home.

# A COLD-AIR BALLOON

Let's grind through the earth in our cold-air balloon!

On down through the ground in our magic cocoon,

We'll burrow like gophers! We'll sink like a stone!

We'll gaze at the world up above us, and moan!

We'll sob in the darkness, we'll cry in the cold

At the slugs and the bugs and the slime and the mold.

As worms wiggle by us in worlds anaerobic

We'll weep and we'll whimper! We'll feel claustrophobic!


And just when we're at our most frightened and nervous,

Right then we'll ascend to the heavenly surface.

We'll soak in the sunlight! We'll breathe in the air!

We'll jump up and down and around without care!

And thanks to our flight in that horrid balloon,

For the rest of our lives, we'll feel high as the moon.

# WHAT?
# YOU THINK
# I HAVE A BAD MEMORY?

Sorry, you're wrong—I *don't* have a bad…

Um, whatever it was you said I had.

# GROWN-UPS ARE BETTER (III)

Everyone sing along with me!

"GROWN-UPS ARE BETTER THAN KIDS!"

Say it together, one, two, three...

"GROWN-UPS ARE BETTER THAN KIDS!"

...

*Excuse me, why aren't you singing along with me?*

...

*What?! You DON'T think grown-ups are better than kids?!*

...

*Well, kid, that's because you're just a KID. You don't know ANYTHING. But grown-ups, such as myself, know lots of things. That's why we're BETTER than kids. So you should do what I say—and I say sing along with me. All righty, then. Ready? Here we go!*

We know it's true! We know it's right!

"GROWN-UPS ARE BETTER THAN KIDS!"

So shout it out with all your might!

"GROWN-UPS ARE..."

...

*Um, I couldn't help but notice that you were once again NOT singing. Maybe you misunderstood me. I didn't say DON'T sing. I said DO sing. Okay? So let's try this one more time or else you're in big trouble and I mean it.*

Come on and shout to all the world!
"GROWN-UPS ARE BETTER THAN—"

*WHY AREN'T YOU SINGING?!?!?!*

*…*

*Okay, okay, okay. Here's the deal: Since you don't believe me, let's try singing the OPPOSITE—"Kids are better than grown-ups!" Then you'll hear how RIDICULOUS it sounds to say that. We'll all sing "Kids are better than grown-ups!" over and over again, and then I KNOW you'll finally agree with me that that's not true. Okay? Let's start!*

KIDS ARE BETTER THAN GROWN-UPS!

KIDS ARE BETTER THAN GROWN-UPS!

KIDS ARE BETTER THAN GROWN-UPS! *Now doesn't that sound silly?*

KIDS ARE BETTER THAN GROWN-UPS! *Crazy, right?*

KIDS ARE BETTER THAN GROWN-UPS!

KIDS ARE BETTER THAN GROWN-UPS! *Okay, I think we can stop now.*

KIDS ARE BETTER THAN GROWN-UPS! *Please stop?*

KIDS ARE BETTER THAN GROWN-UPS! *Stop!!!!*

KIDS ARE BETTER THAN GROWN-UPS!

KIDS ARE BETTER THAN GROWN-UPS! *Oh no. What have I done?*

KIDS ARE BETTER THAN GROWN-UPS…!

KIDS ARE BETTER THAN GROWN-UPS!

# I AM NOT EVEN GOING TO TALK ABOUT THIS NEXT THING

One question I have. On my mind it's been weighing,

And so now I think I'll relay it:

When somebody says something "goes without saying"…

Why do they then go and say it?

# THE NEW BAD WORD

Oh, you've probably heard every word that's obscene,

The curse ones, and worse ones, and those in between.

Perhaps you have read 'em, or even have said 'em;

Forget 'em! I mean it—you might as well shred 'em.

They're old and they're tired, and so uninspired.

It's time to tell all of those words, "Hey! You're fired!"


For now they've come out with a NEW dirty word,

The muddiest, cruddiest word, be assured,

The ugliest, bug-liest, slimy-and-slug-liest,

Not-at-all-snuggliest word that I've heard.


The obscenitists at Obscenities, Inc.

Spent four years perfecting this word's unique stink.

They tested out sounds like "fustunking" and "kwush"

And "wrawnky"—these words would make murderers blush!

They fiddled with consonants, tweaked every vowel,

To maximize outputs of "lowdown" and "foul."

And now that they've figured it out, they've unveiled it—

THE RUDE-CRUDE-AND-LEWDEST WORD EVER (they nailed it!).

So dirty that if in a movie it's stated,

The film would be double-quadruple-R-rated.

And if you dared speak it round Principal Grady?

You'd be in detention till two thousand eighty.


*What* is this word? No, no, I'd never say!

(Well, fine, here's a small hint: it starts with a "K"

And has an "L" in it, but not any "A.")

You know it? You don't. No, it's worse than you think.

I've written it here, in INVISIBLE INK:




To read what it says, soak this book in the tub,

Then bake it, then shake it, then scrub scrub scrub scrub!

The word will appear! (If it doesn't, why then

Simply buy a new copy…and try it again!)

# WORST.
# BIRTHDAY PARTY.
# EVER.

You're right. I shoulda gotta
Piñata.
But I *thought* you said you wanna
*Piranha*.

Now instead of kids taking bites out
Of candy?
The fish did the same thing...
To Mandy.

# SALLY THE CENTIPEDE GETS HER SHOES ON TO TAKE A WALK WITH HER MOM

"Is this the right foot?"
"No," said her mother.
So Sally put it on another.
"Is this the right foot?"
"No," said her mother.
So Sally put it on another.
"Is this the right foot?"
"No," said her mother.
So Sally put it on another.
"Is this the right foot?"
"No," said her mother.
So Sally put it on another.
"Is this the right foot?"
"No," said her mother.
So Sally put it on another.
"Is this the right foot?"
"No," said her mother.
So Sally put it on another.
"Is this the right foot?"
"No," said her mother.
So Sally put it on another.
"Is this the right foot?"
"No," said her mother.
So Sally put it on another.
"Is this the right foot?"
"No," said her mother.
So Sally put it on another.
"Is this the right foot?"
"No," said her mother.
So Sally put it on another.
"Is this the right foot?"
"No," said her mother.
So Sally put it on another.
"Is this the right foot?"
"No," said her mother.
So Sally put it on another.
"Is this the right foot?"
"No," said her mother.
So Sally put it on another.
"Is this the right foot?"
"No," said her mother.

# UNDER MY DRAGON'S WING

Nothing can hurt me,

Nothing can sting,

When I'm hiding under my dragon's wing.


No one can find me,

No one can fight.

Under my dragon's wing, all is all right.


I hear them outside,

Asking, "Where can she be?

Look in the car! Now look in the tree!


Check the gazebo,

Peek in the wagon.

Search everywhere—but don't bother that dragon…"

And they'd never guess
That the dragon's my friend
And I'll hide by his side till the day meets its end.

I feel all his strength
And his warmth and his guile,
And I hear them all calling for me…and I smile.

For no one says "No" here,
And no one tells lies,
And here I can dream and I'm just the right size.

I'm all that I want;
I don't need a thing,
Here at home…under my dragon's wing.

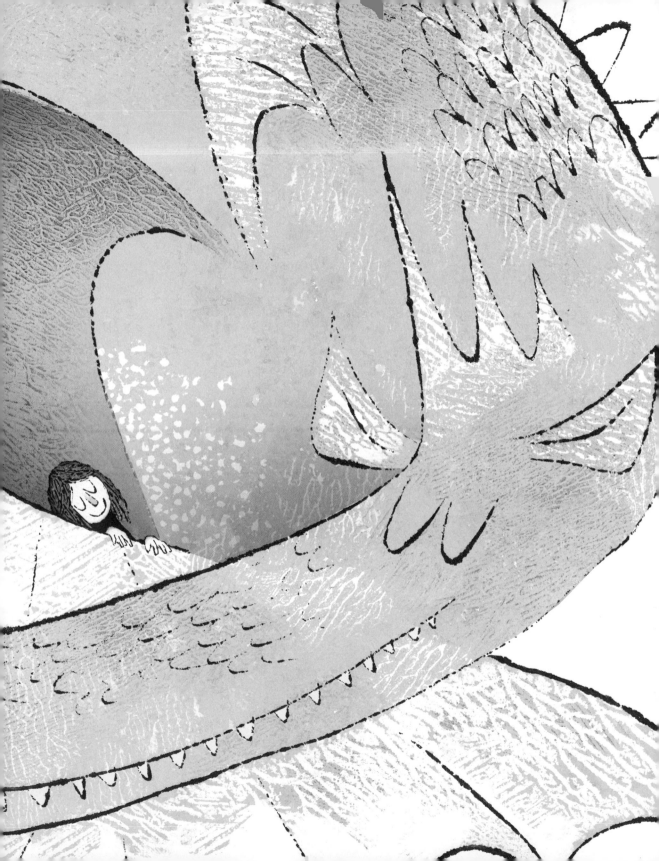

# ON THE OTHER HAND, THEY BOTH HATE DANDELIONS

Mrs. McMarden

Inspected her garden

With great disappointment and dread.

"My fooflower row

Refuses to grow

Among all these funk weeds," she said.

Three houses over
Mrs. McRover
Was sprinkling her garden with seeds.
"I must start from scratch
With my funkflower patch—
Curse all these fooflower weeds!"

# EVEN THE BUTTERFLY

Even the butterfly, monarch of light,

Who toiled all her youth without beauty or flight,

Will often look wistful and longingly say…

"Ah, what I'd give to be young one more day!"

# MORAL: IF IT'S NOT YOUR MAGIC WAND, *LEAVE IT ALONE*

Look! I found a magic wand.

And here's a wizard's hat!

*No, you shouldn't put that on!*

It fits! Now how 'bout that?

Let's make something disappear!

*No! Drop that wand and hat!*

Watch! I'll turn this mirror here

Into a…kitty cat!

*No, no, no, no! Not a mirror!*

*Stop it! Stop it now!*

"Kaladooza kaladeerer,

Kastra mastra—"……meow!

Meow meow meow! Meow! Meow!

*Oh no! Oh no! What a pity!*

Meow! Meow! Meow! Meow!

*My friend is now a kitty!*

Meow meow meow! Meow! Meow!

*Don't you worry now!*

*I'll turn you back someway, somehow!*

Meow. Meow, meow.


*Then again…You're cute like that.*

Meow? MEOW! MEOW!

*I've always wished I had a cat…*

MEOWMEOWMEOWMEOWMEOW!!

*Yes, I'll keep you for my pet!*

MEOW!! MEOW!! MEOW!!

*Stop yelling, or we'll see the vet!*

MEO—Meow.


*That's more like it. Here, have some milk.\**

(shrug) Meow. (lap, lap, lap)

\*That scientist popped up AGAIN with this question:
"Did you know milk's bad for the feline digestion?"
Now cats may be grateful,
But I'm more irateful—
I'm sick of this scientist giving suggestions!

# THE ICE CREAM MONDAE

Have you ever tasted an ice cream *mondae*?
(It's simply a sundae left out overnight.)

It's all warm and melted
Like slime, if you felt it,
And boy, if you smelt it
It wouldn't smell right.

The cream is all crusted,
The cherries are busted,
And you'd be disgusted
At such a sad sight.

So gloppy and goopish,
Primordial soupish.
You'd have to be stupish
For taking a bite.

And yet, though it's icky
And stagnant and sticky,
Just give it a licky,
And hey—it's all right!

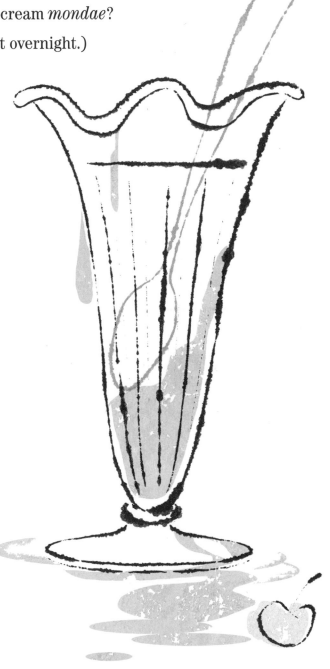

# L-O-V-E

**L** is for Looking out for others.

**O** is for Openheartedness.

**R** is for—

*Hey! There's no "R" in "LOVE"!*

…I know, but I thought maybe I could say that I'm for
Respecting—

*No! No! No! There is no "R" in "LOVE"!! Get outta here, R!
Go on, git!*

*Okay, that's more like it. Now let's keep going.*

**V** is for…Very guilty about how mean we just were to the
letter R.

**G** is for Guys, you can't go around saying that you're all
about love, and then act so terrible to letters that just don't
happen to be in the word, like myself and R.

**P** is for Pretty good argument, G—love should be about accepting everyone, including us!

…

**L** is for Look, we've been doing some thinking, and you're right. The four of us went a little too far, and we're sorry. Please forgive us. All you other letters, come on back!

**E** is for Everyone is welcome now!

And that's what

LORVGPLE

is all about!

# JIGSAW PUZZLE DIFFICULTY CHART

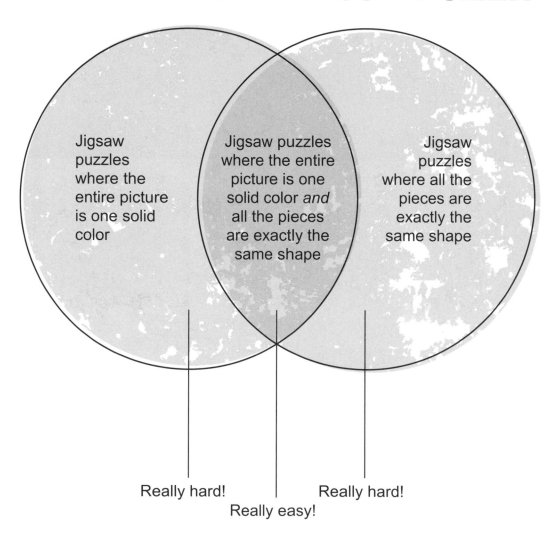

Jigsaw puzzles where the entire picture is one solid color

Jigsaw puzzles where the entire picture is one solid color *and* all the pieces are exactly the same shape

Jigsaw puzzles where all the pieces are exactly the same shape

Really hard!

Really easy!

Really hard!

# THE POEM THAT'S TITLED "THE POEM THAT'S TITLED 'THE POEM THAT'S TITLED 'THE POEM THAT'S TITLED 'THE DOOR'"'"

Read me the poem that's titled "The Poem That's Titled
   'The Poem That's Titled 'The Poem That's Titled 'The Door.'"'"
We'll sit on the chair by the cat on the chair by the cat on the
   chair by the cat on the chair by the cat on the floor,
And just like your dad and his father before and is anyone
   reading this thing anymore and his father before,
You'll read to me some for it's gotten to be quite a bore and
   a chore and I'm starting to snore so

                let's

                  do

                    this

                   no

                  more.

# THE LATEST BEDTIME OF ALL

At six o'clock in deep July,
When late the sun shines bright and hot,
My brother and my friends and I
Were biking round a vacant lot.

Between some two-wheel feats of daring
(Hence the bruise upon my head),
The six of us began comparing
Times we had to go to bed.

Emma said, "My bedtime's eight-ish,
Sometimes half past eight is fine."
Michael laughed, "That's not so late-ish—
*My* bedtime is half till nine."

Sophie crowed, "My bedtime's seven,
But in summer I can choose
To stay up nearly till eleven,
If I watch the local news."

I said, "Nine, so not too early."
Then my older brother, Shawn,
Said, "I've the latest bedtime, surely—
Once I stayed up *until dawn*."

Every kid had finished speaking,
All but little Paul DeVeer.
Paul then piped up, voice near squeaking,
*"I've* the latest bedtime here."

What a joke! We screamed with laughter.
"That's not true," we scoffed at Paul.
How could *his* bedtime be after?
Paul? Up later than us all?

"But it's true!" Paul then did croon,
"Because *my* parents let me stay
Awake all night, morn, afternoon
Till six p.m. on *the next day*!"

As we stood there, stunned and jealous—
What a bedtime! So exciting!—
Paul DeVeer yelled, "See ya, fellas!"
Grabbed his bike and started riding.

"Why're you leaving?" Michael cried.
Paul just stopped and turned his head.
"It's *yesterday's* bedtime *now*," he sighed...
And off he went to go to bed.

# THE LOSER'S CHEER

I won last place!

I won last place!

No one can match me for slowness of pace!

Now maybe you'd say that I stunk in that race,

But I'd rather put on a happier face,

And that's why I say "I'm a Going-Slow Ace!"

So in your face!

I won last place!

# THE CHILD'S FAREWELL

A hug and a kiss,

You're the one that I'll miss.

Oh, how I wish you could stay.

# THE PARENT'S RESPONSE

A kiss and a hug,

I'll miss your mug.

I love you—now have a great day.

# ON MY INTENTIONS OF EXPANDING MY EXPERIENCES EATING GARDEN CUISINE, WITH AN APPROXIMATE TIME FRAME INCLUDED

Someday I'll try a tomato…

Not today, though.

# LET'S MEET RIGHT HERE IN TWENTY-FIVE YEARS

Let's meet right here in twenty-five years.

Promise to come back and visit me then!

Soon you'll outgrow me; our fare-thee-well nears.

This way? I know that I'll see you again.


Through decades divided, I'll be so delighted

In thinking how one day we'll be reunited.

Then, on that day, as you come into view,

I'll say to myself, "Is it you? It *is* you!"

Can you just imagine the grown-up you'll be

In exactly one quarter of one century?

Taller, and wiser, and more self-assured,

Fully-grown-upward and mostly-matured.

Oh, what you'll know then! Oh, how you'll look!

And what about *me*? Oh, well…


I'm just a book.

I'm just a book. I don't grow—it's my curse.

The changes you'll see in me all will be worse:

Dusty, and musty, my jacket in tatters,

Sticky from decades-old grape jelly splatters.

Things that were strong will instead be all brittle.

Things that were smooth will be creased in the middle.

Things will be yellow that used to be white.

Words will be fuzzy. My spine won't be right.

I'll groan when I'm opened (if open I can)…

I'll be the book form of a very old man.


But still, if you will, I'd be thrilled beyond mention,

If that day, you'll pay me a little attention.


Sit down once more with me, see what's within.

Flip through my pages (and possibly grin).

Vaguely remember that cow that tipped over,

Whydoos, and Toby, and Mrs. McRover,

The short anaconda, the one-eyed Orr,

That ongoing thing with the poem "The Door."


You might not enjoy it as much as you'd think—

"The drawings are cool, but these poems? They stink!"

But maybe,

Just maybe,

This book will, somehow,

Remind you of you-long-ago (that's you-now),

And maybe you'll find that the door (yes, *that* door),

That once led all over, now leads to "before,"

And feel for a moment that wonder again:

The charm of your childhood, the tallness of ten,

That yesteryouth lightness that leads us to say,

"Ah, what I'd give to be young one more day!"


And as you stare down, sifting through all my pages,

*I'll* stare back up and think, "Gosh, it's been ages."

For while I'll be older and ravaged by time,

You, you'll be wondrous—and right in your prime.

The living you lived through in twenty-five years

Will shine on your face, from your nose to your ears;

At times you felt lost, but now feel it no longer.

You suffered some heartbreak, but got through it stronger.

Radiant, confident, cool, levelheaded—

You figured your dream out, then set out to get it.

This book will be honored to finally view

The magnificent grown-up that grew up from you.

And seeing your face, that for years went unknown,

And feeling your hands, and how much they'll have grown,

If that's the last ever I'm opened, that night?

Then I'll be okay, for I'll know you're all right.

In twenty-five years, let's meet right here.

Once more, take me down from the shelf.

You'll grow up amazing, that's already clear...

But I want to see for myself.

# UM, YOU CAN STOP READING NOW. THAT WAS THE LAST POEM.

You've read them all, from bad to worse,

Now that's the end to all my verse.

Go play outside. Go eat some cheese.

There's nothing left but indices.

# OOPS, THAT ACCIDENTALLY RHYMED. OKAY, SO *THAT* WAS THE LAST POEM. BUT THERE ARE ABSOLUTELY NO MORE FROM HERE. SO STOP READING.

I'm finished! I'm quitting!

This time? I'm not kidding.

# DARN IT! I'M JUST NO GOOD AT NOT RHYMING. BUT I'M TELLING YOU, THIS IS REALLY THE END!

So

go

away,

okay?

# INDEX* OF TITLES (IN THE BOOK)

*Please read my Author's Note on the copyright page regarding the strange page numbering. Or better yet? Don't. To tell the truth, I'm embarrassed by the whole mess and would rather just completely forget about it.

# OUTDEX (OF TITLES THAT DID NOT MAKE THE FINAL CUT)

# ACKNOWLEDGMENTS

The arrow on the left reads, bottom to top: **Not Very Grateful at All** — **MY LEVEL OF GRATITUDE** — **Extremely Grateful**

—My family. Duh.

—Everyone who helped this become a book: David Miner and Richard Abate, who sold it; Andrea Spooner, who bought it and made it much less terrible; Molly Leach, who made it look pretty; and the rest of Little, Brown and Company. *Especially* Little.

—People who looked at early versions of this book and gave me smart feedback: Kate Montgomery, Jonathan Cohen, and—once again—Silas and Jozy and Hilary.

—Former teachers and mentors of mine, other writers whose books inspired me, and supportive friends. There are far too many to name, so I'll just name one of them: Carl.

—That guy who told me this book would never sell. (It kind of motivated me.)

—If somewhere there is a deep pit full of angry, human-eating frog-monsters …and if one person has to stand guard at all times and knock any frog-monsters who try to escape back to the bottom of the pit…then I'd like to thank that person, because I never would have been able to get much work done with a bunch of frog-monsters around trying to eat me.

—THIS SPACE FOR SALE. The first person to send me one million dollars can get their name here in every other future edition of the book!

—My dear neighbors Mrs. McRover and Mrs. McMarden, who, while they were gardening, gave me the idea for exactly one poem: "The Gecko."

—Lane Smith. I DO NOT LOOK LIKE THAT!!!

—Abraham Lincoln. Yes, he was a great president. But honestly, he was not very helpful to me in terms of writing this book.

—Jon and Christine Arden, who totally messed up the page numbering.

# CHRIS HARRIS

lives in Los Angeles with his family, where he spends his non-rhyming time writing for television. He loves peppermint stick ice cream and, when he's not too full, just a little bit more peppermint stick ice cream but don't tell anyone. In his spare time, he gets older.

If you ever meet Chris, then here's what you should do: Walk up to him and ask him the question, "Shneeple?" while pulling your ear. Chris promises that he will respond by saying, "Shnomple!" and hitting himself on the forehead. In fact, this is something you can do to anyone in the world, too. Ask them, "Shneeple?" Then if they've read this page of the book, they'll answer "Shnomple!" and hit themselves on the forehead. It's like you'll be members of a secret club!

Finally, Chris Harris warns you not to trust anything that Lane Smith has written below. There is at least one glaring lie.

# LANE SMITH

is the *New York Times* bestselling creator of *It's a Book; John, Paul, George & Ben;* and many other favorite children's books, as well as the illustrator of the contemporary classic *The Stinky Cheese Man and Other Fairly Stupid Tales* by Jon Scieszka. Lane has won four *New York Times* Best Illustrated Book awards, three Society of Illustrators medals, two Caldecott Honors, and one Most Beautiful Baby ribbon (second place, 1960). He lives in rural Connecticut with his wife, Molly, his dog Micah, and his cat Lulu. One likes her belly rubbed, one did a brilliant design for this book, and one enjoys chew toys.